ELEPHANT'S STORY

Tracey Campbell Pearson

Margaret Ferguson Books
Farrar Straus Giroux
New York

For Grace

Farrar Straus Giroux Books for Young Readers
175 Fifth Avenue, New York 10010

Copyright © 2013 by Tracey Campbell Pearson
All rights reserved
Color separations by Bright Arts (H.K.) Ltd.
Printed in China by Toppan Leefung Printers Ltd.,
Dongguan City, Guangdong Province
Designed by Jay Colvin
First edition, 2013
3 5 7 9 10 8 6 4 2

mackids.com

Library of Congress Cataloging-in-Publication Data
Pearson, Tracey Campbell, author, illustrator.
    Elephant's story / Tracey Campbell Pearson. — First edition.
        pages cm
    Summary: Elephant finds a book and then sneezes, mixing up
all the letters.
    ISBN 978-0-374-39913-9 (hardcover)
    [1. Books and reading—Fiction.   2. Alphabet—Fiction.
3. Elephants—Fiction.]   I. Title.

PZ7.P323318El 2013
[E]—dc23
                                                            2013000313

Farrar Straus Giroux Books for Young Readers may be purchased for business or promotional use.
For information on bulk purchases please contact Macmillan Corporate and Premium Sales
Department at (800) 221-7945 x5442 or by email at specialmarkets@macmillan.com.

The day Gracie lost her favorite book, Elephant found it.

Sniff, sniff, sniff, and . . . OOPS!
The words went up his trunk.

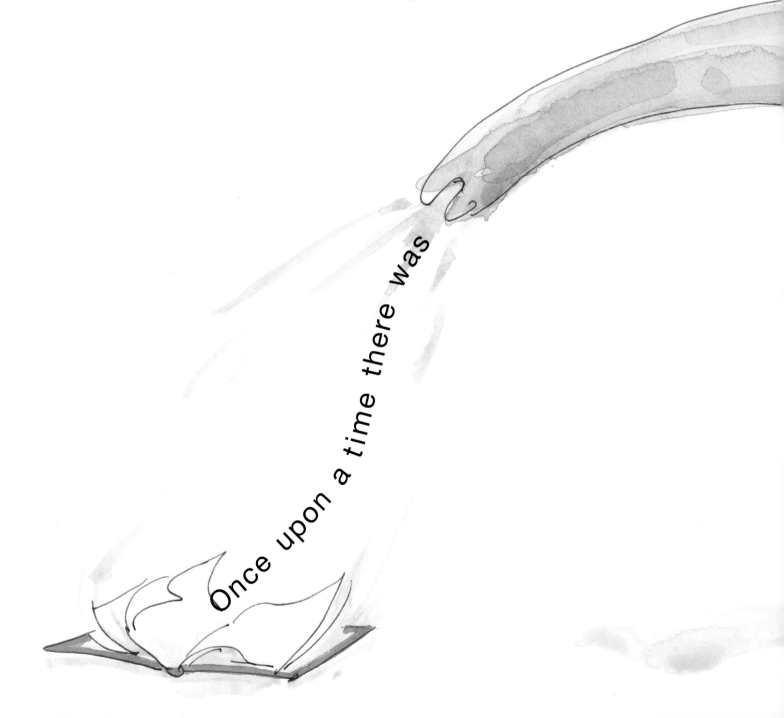

Once upon a time there was

They wiggled and jiggled and squiggled inside.
Elephant sneezed.
AH . . . AHH . . . AHHH . . . CHOOOOO!

Letters flew everywhere.

Elephant tried to put the letters back into words,
but they were all mixed up.
He went to his friends for help.

Alligator wanted to eat the letters.

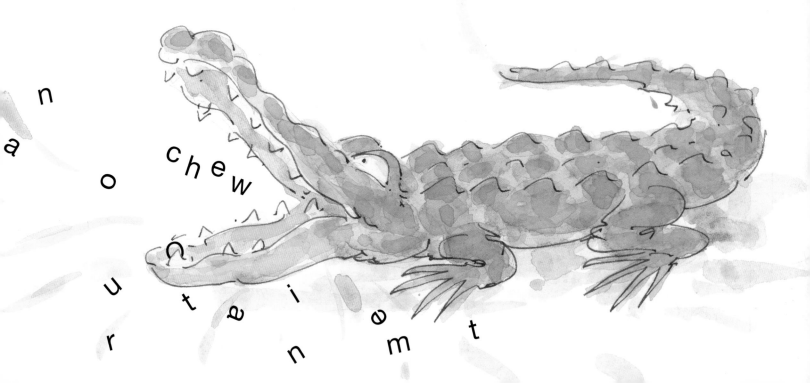

Seal wanted to juggle the letters.

The monkeys wanted to toss the letters.

Bear just wanted to sleep.

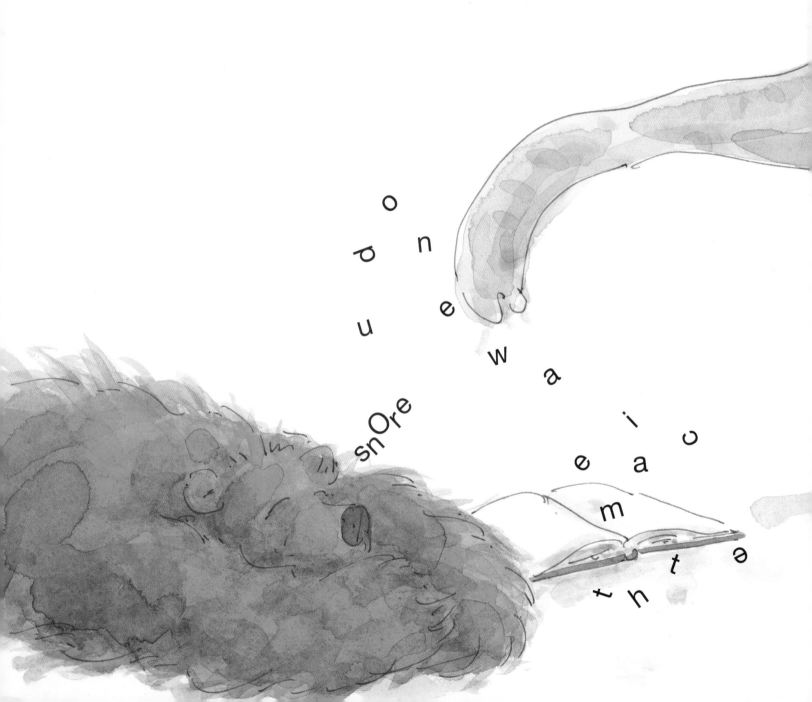

Poor Elephant. His friends were no help at all.
He sniffed the letters back into his trunk and went home.

Along came Gracie. She was looking for her book.
There it was. Elephant was sitting on it.

Gracie looked at the empty book. She looked at Elephant.
"Where are my words?" she asked.

Gracie pulled and pulled and pulled.

When that didn't work, she tickled his trunk.

Elephant sneezed.
AH . . . AHH . . . AHHH . . . CHOOOOO!
He showered Gracie with letters.

Gracie showed Elephant how to make the letters into words. Together, they put the words back in the book.

time

was

Once

there

upon a

Then Gracie read the words to Elephant: "Once upon a time there was"—and she added some of her own—"a girl called Gracie, who made a new friend. His name was Elephant."